Praise for

WEIGHT

'Jeanette Winterson creates an uncategorisable, meditative and moving book.'

David Mitchell, *Sunday Herald* (Glasgow)

'Winterson focuses on Atlas's bamboozlement by Heracles . . . with promiscuous wit and exuberant fantasy.'

The Independent (UK)

Praise for THE MYTHS SERIES

'An ambitious new project to reinterpret the world's most lasting stories.' *The Globe and Mail*

'One of the most ambitious acts of mass storytelling in recent years and one that transcends racial and historical borders.' *Metro* (UK)

'A feat of mythic proportions.' *The Los Angeles Times*

'This is powerful stuff and sets the bar very high. . . . The concept is valuable and valid.'

The New York Times Book Review

Also by Jeanette Winterson

Lighthousekeeping (2004)
The PowerBook (2000)
The World and Other Places (short stories) (1998)
Gut Symmetries (1997)
*Art & Lies: A Piece for Three Voices
and a Bawd* (1994)
Written on the Body (1992)
Sexing the Cherry (1989)
The Passion (1987)
Boating for Beginners (1985)
Oranges Are Not the Only Fruit (1985)

Myths are universal and timeless stories that reflect and shape our lives – they mirror our desires, our fears, our longings, and provide narratives that attempt to help us make sense of the world. The Myths series brings together some of the finest writers of our time to provide a contemporary take on our most enduring stories. Authors in the series also include Chinua Achebe, Margaret Atwood, Karen Armstrong, A.S. Byatt, David Grossman, Milton Hatoum, Natsuo Kirino, Alexander McCall Smith, Victor Pelevin, Ali Smith, Donna Tartt and Su Tong.

WEIGHT

Jeanette Winterson

Vintage Canada

VINTAGE CANADA EDITION, 2006

Copyright © 2005 Jeanette Winterson
Published by agreement with Canongate Books Ltd, Edinburgh, Scotland

Published in Canada by Vintage Canada, a division of Random House of Canada Limited, Toronto, in 2006. Originally published in hardcover in Canada by Alfred A. Knopf Canada, a division of Random House of Canada Limited, Toronto, and simultaneously in Great Britain and the United States of America by Canongate Books Ltd, Edinburgh, New York and Melbourne, in 2005. Distributed by Random House of Canada Limited, Toronto.

www.randomhouse.ca

Library and Archives Canada Cataloguing in Publication

Winterson, Jeanette
        Weight : the myth of Atlas and Heracles / Jeanette Winterson.

(The myths series)
ISBN-13: 978-0-676-97423-2
ISBN-10: 0-676-97423-6

1. Atlas (Greek deity)—Fiction. 2. Heracles (Greek mythology)—Fiction.
I. Title. II. Series: Myths series.

PR6073.I558W44 2006   823'.914   C2006-902079-5

Text and logo design © Pentagram

Typeset in Van Dijck by Palimpsest Book Production Ltd, Polmont, Stirlingshire

Printed and bound in Canada

10 9 8 7 6 5 4 3 2 1

For Deborah Warner, who lifted the weight.

Sedimentary rock is formed over vast expanses of time, as layer upon layer of sediment is deposited on the sea bottom.

Being formed in this way, such rock is usually arranged in a succession of horizontal bands, or strata, with the oldest strata lying at the bottom.

Each band will often contain the fossilised remains of the plants and animals that died at the time at which the sediment was originally laid down.

The strata of sedimentary rock are like the pages of a book, each with a record of contemporary life written on it. Unfortunately, the record is far from complete. The process of sedimentation in any one place is invariably interrupted by new periods in which sediment is not laid down, or existing sediment is eroded. The succession of layers is further obscured as strata become twisted or folded, or even completely inverted by enormous geological forces, such as those involved in mountain building ...

The strata of sedimentary rock are like the pages of a book ...

Each with a record of contemporary life written on it ...

Unfortunately the record is far from complete ...

The record is far from complete ...

CONTENTS

Introduction xiii

I want to tell the story again I
Weight of the World 9
Heracles 27
Thought-Wasp 47
Three Golden Apples 63
No Way Out . . . 77
But Through 85
Leaning on the Limits of Myself 95
Private Mars IOI
Hero of the World IO7
Woof! I2I
Boundaries I29
Desire I35
I want to tell the story again I47

Introduction

Choice of subject, like choice of lover, is an intimate decision.

Decision, the moment of saying yes, is prompted by something deeper; recognition. I recognise you; I know you again, from a dream or another life, or perhaps even from a chance sighting in a café, years ago.

These chance sightings, these portents, these returns, begin the unconscious connection with the subject, an unconscious connection that waits for an ordinary moment of daylight to show its face.

When I was asked to choose a myth to write about, I realised I had chosen already. The story of Atlas holding up the world was in my mind before the telephone call had ended. If the call had not come, perhaps I would never have written the story, but when the call did come, that story was waiting to be written.

Re-written. The recurring language motif of *Weight* is 'I want to tell the story again.'

My work is full of Cover Versions. I like to take stories we think we know and record them differently. In the re-telling comes a new emphasis or bias, and the new arrangement of the key elements demands that fresh material be injected into the existing text.

Weight moves far away from the simple story of Atlas's punishment and his temporary relief when Hercules takes the world off his shoulders. I wanted to explore loneliness, isolation, responsibility, burden, and freedom too, because my version has a very particular end not found elsewhere.

Of course I wrote it directly out of my own situation. There is no other way.

Weight has a personal story broken against the bigger story of the myth we know and the myth

I have re-told. I have written this personal story in the First Person, indeed almost all of my work is written in the First Person, and this leads to questions of autobiography.

Autobiography is not important. Authenticity is important. The writer must fire herself through the text, be the molten stuff that welds together disparate elements. I believe there is always exposure, vulnerability, in the writing process, which is not to say it is either confessional or memoir. Simply, it is real.

Right now, human beings as a mass, have a gruesome appetite for what they call 'real', whether it's Reality TV or the kind of plodding fiction that only works as low-grade documentary, or at the better end, the factual programmes and biographies and 'true life' accounts that occupy the space where imagination used to sit.

Such a phenomenon points to a terror of the inner life, of the sublime, of the poetic, of the non-material, of the contemplative.

Against all this, a writer such as myself, who believes in the power of story telling for its mythic and not its explanatory qualities, and who believes that language is much more than information, must row against the tide rather like Siegfried rowing against the current of the Rhine.

The Myth series is a marvellous way of telling stories — re-telling stories for their own sakes, and finding in them permanent truths about human nature. All we can do is keep telling the stories, hoping that someone will hear. Hoping that in the noisy echoing nightmare of endlessly breaking news and celebrity gossip, other voices might be heard, speaking of the life of the mind and the soul's journey.

Yes, I want to tell the story again.

I want to tell the story again

The free man never thinks of escape.

In the beginning there was nothing. Not even space and time. You could have thrown the universe at me and I would have caught it in one hand. There was no universe. It was easy to bear.

This happy nothing ended fifteen aeons ago. It was a strange time, and what I know is told to me in radioactive whispers; that's all there is left of one great shout into the silence.

What is it that you contain? The dead. Time. Light patterns of millennia opening in your gut. Every minute, in each of you, a few million potassium atoms succumb to radioactive decay. The energy that powers these tiny atomic events has been locked inside potassium atoms ever since a star-sized bomb exploded nothing into being. Potassium, like uranium and radium, is a long-lived radioactive nuclear waste of the supernova bang that accounts for you.

Your first parent was a star.

It was hot as hell in those days. It was Hell, if hell is where the life we love cannot exist. Those cease-less burning fires and volcanic torments are lodged in us as ultimate fear. The hells we invent are the hells we have known. Hell is; *was not*, *is not*, *cannot*. Science calls it the world before life began – the Hadean period. But life had begun, because life is more than the ability to reproduce. In the molten lava spills and cratered rocks, life longed for life. *The proto, the almost, the maybe.* Not Venus. Not Mars. Earth.

Planet Earth, that wanted life so badly, she got it.

Moving forward a few billion years, there was a mira-cle. At least that's what I call the unexpected fact that changes the story. Earth had bacterial life, but no oxygen, and oxygen was a deadly poison. Then, in a quiet revolution as explosive in its own way as a star, a new kind of bacteria, cyanobacteria started to photosynthesise – and a bi-product of photosynthesis is oxygen. Planet earth had a new atmosphere. The rest is history.

Well not quite. I could list for you the wild optimism of the Cambrian era, pushing up mountains like grass grows daisies, or the Silurian dream-days of starfish and gastropods. About 400 million years ago, shaking salt water from their fins and scales, the first land animals climbed out of the warm lagoons of the vast coral reefs. The Triassic and Jurassic periods belong to the dinosaurs, efficient murder weapons, common as nightmares. Then three or four million years ago – chancy and brand new – what's this come here – a mammoth and something like a man?

★   ★   ★

The earth was amazed. Earth was always strange and new to herself. She never anticipated what she would do next. She never guessed the coming wonder. She loved the risk, the randomness, the lottery probability of a winner. We forget, but she never did, that what we take for granted is the success story. The failures have disappeared. This planet that seems so obvious and inevitable is the jackpot. Earth is the blue ball with the winning number on it.

Make a list. Look around you. *Rock, sand, soil, fruit trees, roses, spiders, snails, frogs, fish, cattle, horses, rainfall, sunshine, you and me.* This is the grand experiment called life. What could be more unexpected?

All the stories are here, silt-packed and fossil-stored. The book of the world opens anywhere, chronology is one method only and not the best. Clocks are not time. Even radioactive rock-clocks, even gut-spun DNA, can only tell time like a story.

When the universe exploded like a bomb, it started ticking like a bomb too. We know our sun will die, in another hundred million years or so, then the lights will go out and there will be no light to read by any more.

'Tell me the time' you say. And what you really say is 'Tell me a story.'

Here's one I haven't been able to put down.

Weight of the World

My father was Poseidon. My mother was the Earth.

My father loved the strong outlines of my mother's body. He loved her demarcations and her boundaries. He knew where he stood with her. She was solid, certain, shaped and material.

My mother loved my father because he recognised no boundaries. His ambitions were tidal. He swept, he sank, he flooded, he re-formed. Poseidon was a deluge of a man. Power flowed off him. He was deep, sometimes calm, but never still.

My mother and father teemed with life. They *were* life. Creation depended on them and had done so before there was air or fire. They sustained so much. They were so much. To each other they were irresistible.

Both were volatile. My father obviously so, my

mother more alarmingly. She was serene as a rock but volcano'd with anger. She was quiet as a desert but tectonically challenged. When my mother threw a plate across the room, the whole world felt the crash. My father could be whipped into a storm in moments. My mother grumbled and growled and shook for days or weeks or months until her rage fissured and crumpled entire cities or forced human kind into lava-like submission.

Humankind . . . They never could see it coming. Look at Pompeii. There they are in the bathouses, sitting in their chairs, wearing skeletal looks of charred surprise.

When my father wooed my mother she lapped it up. He was playful, he was warm, he waited for her in the bright blue shallows and came a little closer, then drew back, and his pull was to leave a little gift on her shore; a piece of coral, mother of pearl, a shell as spiralled as a dream.

Sometimes he was a long way out and she missed

him and the beached fishes gasped for breath. Then he was all over her again, and they were mermaids together, because there was always something feminine about my father, for all his power. Earth and water are the same kind, just as fire and air are their opposites.

She loved him because he showed her to herself. He was her moving mirror. He took her round the world, the world that she was, and held it up for her to see, her beauty of forests and cliffs and coastlines and wild places. To him she was both paradise and fear and he loved both. Together they went where no human had ever been. Places only they could go, places only they could be. Wherever he went, she was there; a gentle restraint, a serious reminder; *the earth and the waters that covered the earth*. He knew though, that while he could not cover the whole of her, she underpinned the whole of him. For all his strength, she was strong.

I was born. I was born one of the Titans, half man, half god, a giant of a giant race. I was born on an island where my father could lie over my mother for a day and a night before subsiding. From this prolonged intercourse, riddling himself into every crack, I was bound to be a fatal combination of them both. I am as turbulent as my father. I am as brooding as my mother. I act suddenly. I never forget. I sometimes forgive, compassion washing away memory. I know what love is. I know love's counterfeit. At the same time, my good nature makes me easy to deceive. Like my brother Prometheus, I have been punished for overstepping the mark. He stole fire. I fought for freedom.

Boundaries, always boundaries.

I keep telling the story again and though I find different exits, the walls never fall. My life is paced out – here and here and here – I can alter its shape but I can't get beyond it. I tunnel through, seem to find a way out, but the exits lead nowhere. I'm back inside, leaning on the limits of myself.

This is the body, the sealed unit that cautiously

takes in what it needs to survive, that stoutly repels invaders of the microbe kind. This is the body, whose boundaries weaken only in decay and then the freedom it brings is useless. United with the world at last, I am dead to it.

This is the body, and my body is the world in little. I am the Kosmos – the all that there is, and at the same time I was never more outside, never more than nothing. Nothing bounded by nothing.

Nothing has an unlikely property. *It is heavy*.

The story is a simple one. I had a farm. I had cattle. I had a vineyard. I had daughters. I lived on Atlantis, the perfect synthesis of a wealthy mother and a proud father. The Titans bowed to no-one, not even Zeus, whose thunderbolts were like a game to us.

When I wanted gold and jewels I asked my mother where she kept them and she indulged me as mothers indulge sons, and showed me her secret mines and underground caves.

When I wanted whales or harbours or nets lined with fish or pearls for my daughters, I went to my father, who respected me and treated me as an equal. I dived with him into hot springs that blasted the floor of the ocean. We swam wrecks and tamed porpoises. Land and sea were equal home to me, and when Atlantis was finally destroyed, I even felt a kind of gladness. All that loss was after all, only my mother and father's embrace. I was nothing. I returned to nothing. I wish it had been so.

Boundaries, always boundaries, and the longing for infinite space.

I built a walled garden, a *temenos*, a sacred space. I lifted the huge stones with my own hands and piled them carefully, as a goatherd would, leaving tiny gaps to let the wind through. A solid wall is easily collapsed. My mother stirring in her sleep could do as much. A wall well built with invisible spaces will allow the winds that rage against it to pass through. When the earth underneath it trembles, the spaces make room for movement and settlement. The wall stands. The wall's strength is not in the stones but in the spaces between the stones. It's a joke against me I think, that for all my strength and labour, the wall relies on nothing. *Write it more substantially –* NOTHING.

This garden is well known. My daughters, the Hesperides, tend it, and far and wide it is called *The Garden of the Hesperides*. Along with the usual kinds of fruit, the garden enjoys a rarity. My mother, Mother Earth gave the goddess Hera a golden apple tree for her wedding day, and Hera loved the tree so much that she asked me to tend it for her.

I have heard some men say that the apples are solid gold, and that this is the reason why they must be guarded so carefully. Every man assumes that what is valuable to himself must be coveted by others.

Men who love gold, long for gold and guard it with their lives, though life is more precious than any metal. My mother has no need of gold, and what does Hera want with gold? No, the beauty of the tree is in its living nature. Its apples are tiny, pineapple-scented jewels that hang from fruiting branches covered in dark green leaves. There is no other tree like it. It stands in the centre of the garden, and once a year, Hera comes to collect its harvest.

All well and good. At least I thought so until Hera appeared to me in a rage that sent me cowering inside a shed of excuses.

My daughters had been secretly eating the sacred fruit. Who could blame them, the tree, sweet-scented and heavy, and the grass underneath it wet with evening dew? Their feet were bare and their mouths were eager. They are girls after all.

I did not see the harm myself, but the gods are jealous of their belongings. Hera sent the serpent Ladon to guard the tree, and there he is now, coiled and watchful, with a hundred heads and double that in tongues. I hate him, though he is a dark dream of my mother's, a solid nightmare birthed into day.

When I was cast out of the garden, I thought nothing heavier could befall me.

I was wrong.

The war between the gods and the Titans was a war we had preferred to avoid. There are several versions of this war. One thing is certain; what began as just cause became just excuse. We fought for ten years.

Some say that my father was Uranus and that my brothers and I, especially Cronus, plotted to attack him and castrate him. It is certain that Cronus cut off the genitals of Uranus, and then took power himself. It is certain too, that Cronus bore a child, Zeus, who likewise dethroned his father and gained control of the heavens. Zeus had two brothers, Hades and Poseidon, and while Zeus became Lord of the

Sky, Poseidon had his kingdom in the waves, and Hades was content with what lies beneath. The earth was left to mankind.

It was mankind who attacked quiet Atlantis, and Zeus who helped them to destroy my people. I escaped, and joined the revolt against the heavens. I was the war-leader, the one who had lost most and had little to fear. What can a man fear with nothing to lose?

In the long fighting, most of us were killed, and my mother, out of her secret nature, promised victory to Zeus. What Titans were left were banished to Britain, where the cold inhospitable rocks are worse than death. I was spared for my great strength.

In a way I was allowed to be my own punishment.

Because I loved the earth. Because the seas of the earth held no fear for me. Because I had learned the positions of the planets and the track of the stars. Because I am strong, my punishment was to support the Kosmos on my shoulders. I took up the burden of the whole world, the heavens above it, and the depths below. All that there is, is mine, but none of it in my control. This is my monstrous burden. The boundary of what I am.

And my desire?

Infinite space.

It was the day of my punishment.

The gods assembled. The women were on the left and the men were on the right. There's Artemis, worked muscle and tied-back hair, fiddling with her bow so that she doesn't have to look at me. We were friends. We hunted together.

There's Hera, sardonic, aloof. She couldn't care less. As long as it's not her.

There's Hermes, fidgety and pale, he hates trouble. Next to him lounges Hephastus, ill-tempered and lame, Hera's crippled son, tolerated for his gold smithy. Opposite him is Aphrodite his wife, who loathes his body. We've all had her, though we treat her like a virgin. She smiled at me. She was the only one who dared . . .

Zeus read out his decree. *Atlas, Atlas, Atlas*. It's in my name, I should have known. My name is Atlas — it means 'the long suffering one'.

I bent my back and braced my right leg, kneeling with my left. I bowed my head and held my hands, palms up, almost like surrender. I suppose it was surrender. Who is strong enough to escape their fate? Who can avoid what they must become?

The word given, teams of horses and oxen began to strain forward, dragging the Kosmos behind them like a disc-plough. As the great ball ploughed infinity, pieces of time were dislodged. Some fell to earth, giving the gift of prophecy and second sight. Some were thrown out into the heavens, making black holes where past and future cannot be distinguished. Time spattered my calf muscles and the sinews in my thighs. I felt the world before it began, and the future marked me. I would always be here.

As the Kosmos came nearer, the heat of it scorched my back. I felt the world settle against the sole of my foot.

Then, without any sound, the heavens and the earth were rolled up over my body and I supported them on my shoulders.

I could hardly breathe. I could not raise my head. I tried to shift slightly or to speak. I was dumb and still as a mountain. Mount Atlas they soon called me, not for my strength but for my silence.

There was a terrible pain in the seventh vertebra of my neck. The soft tissue of my body was already hardening. The hideous vision of my life was robbing me of life. Time was my Medusa. Time was turning me to stone.

I do not know how long I crouched like this, petrified and motionless.

*   *   *

At last I began to hear something.

I found that where the world was close to my ears, I could hear everything. I could hear conversation, parrots squawking, donkeys braying. I heard the rushing of underground rivers and the crackle of fires lighted. Each sound became a meaning, and soon I began to de-code the world.

Listen, here is a village with a hundred people in it, and at dawn they take their cattle to the pastures and at evening they herd them home. A girl with a limp takes the pails over her shoulders. I know she limps by the irregular clank of the buckets. There's a boy shooting arrows – thwack! thwack! into the padded hide of the target. His father pulls the stopper out of a wine jar.

Listen, there's an elephant chased by a band of men. Over there, a nymph is becoming a tree. Her sighs turn into sap.

Someone is scrambling up a scree slope. His boots loosen the ground under him. His nails are torn. He falls exhausted on some goat-grass. He breathes heavily and goes to sleep.

I can hear the world beginning. Time plays itself back for me. I can hear the ferns uncurling from their tight rest. I can hear pools bubbling with life. I realise I am carrying not only this world, but all possible worlds. I am carrying the world in time as well as in space. I am carrying the world's mistakes and its glories. I am carrying its potential as well as what has so far been realised.

As the dinosaurs crawl through my hair and volcanic eruptions pock my face, I find I am become a part of what I must bear. There is no longer Atlas and the world, there is only the World Atlas. Travel me and I am continents. I am the journey you must make.

Listen, there's a man telling a story about the man who holds the world on his shoulders. Everybody laughs. Only drunks and children will believe that.

*　*　*

No man believes what he does not feel to be true. I should like to unbelieve myself. I sleep at night and wake in the morning hoping to be gone. It never happens. One knee forward, one knee bent, I bear the world.

Heracles

Heracles stepped out of the shadows where he had been listening.

Here he comes, the Hero of the World, wearing a lion-skin and swinging his olive club.

'Have a drink Atlas, you old globe. We've all got our burdens to bear. Your punishment is to hold up the universe. My punishment is to work for a wanker.'

'And who's to blame?' said Atlas. 'Not your father Zeus, but your foster-mother, Hera.'

'Call it Fate not blame,' said Heracles. 'Your name means "long-suffering" mine means "Glory of Hera", which is a bit of a liberty under the circumstances. Does any woman feel love for her husband's bastards? I am son of my father Zeus, but my mother Alceme was mortal. Hera was deceived into suckling me. She's not happy about that. Women don't like a stranger at the tit.'

'She sent a serpent to kill you.'

'I strangled it in my cot. I was too young to bear a grudge.'

'And then she drove you to madness.'

'There's plenty of men been driven to madness by a woman.'

'Only a madman would come here.'

'I need your help.'

Help. He comes for help at the hinge of the world. Heaven and earth fold away from each other, but here they lie edge to edge. To this doubleness he comes for help, this man of double nature, the god in him folded back in human flesh.

'What kind of help?'

'It's a long story.'

'I'm not going anywhere.'

'Well,' said Heracles, 'If you've got all the time in the world, I'll begin.'

Men are unfaithful by nature. This is not a fault in men, for nature should not be accused of faulty workmanship. It is as useless to rail against man's infidelity as it is to complain that water is wet. What god or man is content with what he has? And if he were content, then he is less than god or man.

Alceme was beautiful, so Zeus dressed himself up as her husband and had a quick word with the moon and he got Alceme into bed for a night that lasted thirty-six hours. He gave her pleasure and pleasure grew into a son. To save me from Hera's marital wrath, he tricked her into suckling me just once, and so I gained immortality. Hera can hurt me but she cannot truly harm me. What she really likes to do is humiliate me.

Even a goddess is still a woman.

I was a bit of a braggart in my youth – killed

everything, shagged what was left, and ate the rest. Then Hera made up her mind to drive me mad, and while I was mad, I slit six of my own children, which I regret, and a tent full of other people whose names I didn't even know. Not good behaviour, Atlas, and I always had my standards, even when drunk, so I went to Delphi to try and get forgiveness. The pythoness at Delphi ordered me to make myself servant to Eurystheus. Yes, that slack-prick, gnat-witted, wine-sour Eurystheus. As an atonement, you understand. For twelve years I must do whatever he asks. No matter that he is weak and I am strong. No matter that I could kill him by spitting on him. He is my master. For his glory I have already killed the Nemean Lion, destroyed the Hydra, caught the golden hind of Artemis, captured the world's biggest boar, cleaned the Augean stables, driven away the man-eating Stymphalian birds, coralled the Cretan bull, tamed the carnivorous mares of Diomedes, stripped Hippolyte's Amazon girdle from her body, fetched home the Geryon cattle, and now I find myself here with you, for the eleventh of my labours.

Fruit.

Didn't I say she wanted to humiliate me? What kind of a hero chases after fruit?

You see, Atlas, my old mountain, my old mate, I have to get hold of some of Hera's apples – the special ones she got as a present from your Ma when she married Zeus. They're in your orchard, aren't they? Have you still got the key? You didn't leave it with those bloody Hesperides did you? I don't fancy smarming your daughters, Atlas, I'm strictly off women at the moment – got to concentrate, you know. By the way, just as a bit of gossip, your other daughter Calypso has got that idiot Odysseus in her den and will she let him go? No she won't. Hera herself can't get him away. Odysseus is slippery as a greased boar but Calypso has hands like skewers. They are a bunch, your girls, I must say. You should get them married off.

But to the point, Atlas. If you *have* got the key, would you mind just popping down there and picking one or two, well three, as it happens, three golden apples for your old friend Heracles? I'll take the world off your shoulders while you go. Now there's a handsome offer.

Atlas was silent. Heracles slit a skin of wine and slung it at him, watching the giant's face while they drank. Heracles was a bastard and a blagger, but he was the only man alive who could relieve Atlas of his burden. They both knew that.

'Ladon lies curled round the apple tree,' said Atlas. 'I fear him.'

'What, that poxy snake? That hundred-headed whodunit? Every tongue a question, every answer a hiss of nothing. Ladon's not a monster, he's a tourist attraction.'

'I fear him,' said Atlas.

'Let me tell you,' said Heracles, 'I've faced a lot

worse than Ladon. The Hydra, now she *was* a worm. Chop off one head and straight away there'd be another glaring at you. Like marriage really. And after this I've got to go down into Hell and drag out that stupid dog, what's his name Cerberus? Three heads, loads of teeth – that one. No wonder the dead don't get any letters; who's going to deliver them with a dog like that at the gate? I'll fix him though, just like I fixed the Cretan bull. You've got to look them in the eye Atlas, show 'em who's boss.'

'Ladon has two hundred eyes,' said Atlas.

'Two thousand, two million, I'm Heracles, don't worry about it. I'll go and kill him and bring us something to eat on the way back.'

There he goes, the hero of the world, thick-cut as his olive-club. Is he a joke or a god? His doubleness is his strength and his downfall. He is a joke and a god. One or the other will be the death of him. Which is it?

★   ★   ★

Heracles vaulted the wall into the Garden of the Hesperides. He had the key, but the lock was rusted and he thought it unwise to use his thug-trough manners on Atlas's property.

The garden was thick and overgrown. Heracles trampled through it towards the shining centre, where Hera's tree was rich with fruit.

Ladon was under the tree. Ladon curled like a worm-cast. Ladon, a dragon with a man's tongue. Ladon, a man turned reptile, cold-blooded and morose.

Heracles hailed Ladon.

'Is that you, you bag of venom?'

Ladon opened sixty-five of his eyes but did not stir.

'Don't play dead with me Ladon. Look lively.'

There was a ripple. Small music of Ladon's scales. At his head, he was heavy-sounded as a cymbal, but towards his tail, where the scales were smaller and higher, he was a chime or a triangle. He tinkled at Heracles.

'The girls haven't done much mowing, have they?'

observed our hero, looking at the grass, tall as a tower. 'No one's been here for ages.'

'I live alone,' said Ladon.

'I don't live anywhere,' said Heracles. 'I've been on the road for years now.'

'I heard,' said Ladon.

'Oh, what have you heard?' said Heracles, trying to sound casual.

'That you have offended the gods.'

'That's an overstatement,' said Heracles. 'Hera doesn't like me. That's all.'

'She hates you,' said Ladon.

'All right. She hates me. So what?'

'This is her tree. These are her apples.'

'That's what I've come for.'

'You will be cursed.'

'I'm cursed already. How bad can it get?'

'Go home, Heracles.'

'There is no home.'

★   ★   ★

Ladon reared up, and with his terrible bulk began to uncoil from the sacred tree. His hundred mouths dripped venom. His eyes flashed prophecy. Heracles knew that it would be this poison or the one after. He had taken milk from Hera's breast and she would one day return it to him as poison. He had known as much when he was a baby sleeping on his mother's fleece, and Hera had sent the azure serpent to kill him. This he had strangled, and he had avoided cups and libations ever since. He had defeated the Hydra. He would defeat Ladon. He would not die today. But he knew he would die. Sometimes he thought it was a strange life, this life of avoiding death.

Heracles used the overgrown garden to hide himself from Ladon's angry searching. As the serpent slithered through the long grass and over the unused trellises and frames, Heracles retreated further and further from the centre, towards the wall, where he had left his bow and arrow.

He strung the bow and braced his feet.

'Over here, Ladon, you creep!'

The serpent reared up and as he did so, exposed his soft throat to Heracles' arrow. The flint pierced him and he died at once, his lidless eyes filming over, his jaw-plates sagging.

Heracles knew that all serpents feign death to avoid capture, so he cautiously walked around Ladon's body and hacked off a piece of his armoured tail. The scales were thick as a breastplate, but Heracles wore no armour, only the skin of the Nemean lion that he had slain so easily so long ago.

Caught in a moment's thought between death and death, Heracles did not see Hera standing before him. He suddenly felt a drop of rain against the sweat of his skin. He looked up. She was there. His tormentor and his dream.

Hera was beautiful. She was so beautiful that even a thug like Heracles wished he had shaved. Without a mirror she showed him to himself, muscle-swollen and scarred. He feared her and desired her. His prick kept filling and deflating like a pair of fire bellows. He wanted to rape her but he didn't dare. Her eyes were all contempt and mild disgust.

'Must you kill everything, Heracles?'

'Kill or be killed. Don't blame me.'

'Whom else should I blame?'

'Blame yourself, drop dead gorgeous, all this starts with you.'

'All this started with my husband's trickery and your brutality.'

'You drove me mad.'

'I did not ask you to kill your own children.'

'A mad man has no reason in his head.'

'A brutal man has no pity in his heart.'

'You are my fate, Hera, and guess what? I am yours.'

'A god has no fate. You will never be immortal, Heracles, you are too much a man.'

'You suckled me, and my father is Zeus. That makes me immortal enough.'

'Enough is not enough. I could kill you now.'

'Then kill me. Do you think I'm frightened?'

'You must bring about your own ruin, Heracles.'

'But you'll be there to help me to it, won't you, Hera?'

'If I seem like fate to you, it is because you have no power of your own.'

'No man was ever stronger.'

'No man was ever weaker than you.'

'You talk in riddles, like a woman.'

'Then I will speak plainly, like a man. No hero can be destroyed by the world. His reward is to destroy himself. Not what you meet on the way, but what you are, will destroy you, Heracles.'

Hera moved forward, and delicate as she was, hair shining, her limbs pale, she picked up Ladon light as a toy, and threw him into the heavens where she set him forever as the constellation of the serpent.

The effort had bared her breasts.

'Well then, Heracles, why do you not take the apples?'

Heracles moved forward and with his finger he touched Hera's nipple. He felt it harden, and wetting his fingertip, he touched it again, rubbing around the aureole with his thumb. He wanted to suck her breasts.

Hera put her hand over his. 'Take the apples, Heracles.'

He remembered. He stepped back. Dark-hearted Hera was smiling at him. He had been warned not to pick the apples himself. He must leave them on the tree. Someone else must do his gathering for him.

He stepped back. Her breasts were bare. Why not die now, take the inevitable with some pleasure? He could have her, force his prick in her, and then she'd kill him. He'd die in the cave of her hatred, but she'd feel him die. She'd feel the last pulse of him inside her.

He dropped his hand to his prick and started to masturbate. She watched him, rough and practised, beat himself off in a dozen quick strokes. As he started to come, she kissed him once on the mouth and walked away.

Night.

Ladon's imprint was still in the grass. His image was bright among the stars. Heracles was sitting alone under the sacred tree. He no longer understood the journey, or rather he understood there *was* a journey. Until today he had gone about each task unconcerned by the one before or the one after. He had met the challenge and moved on. He did what he had to do, no more, no less. It was his fate. Fate could not be questioned or considered.

Today was different. Today, for the first time in his life, he thought about what he was doing. He thought about who he was.

Ladon had told him to go home. What if he did?

What if he walked out of the garden and turned away. He could find a ship, change his name. He could leave Heracles behind, an imprint in time, like Ladon, that would fade as the grass grew.

What if he bent the future as easily as an iron bar? Could he not bend himself out of his fate, and leave fate to curve elsewhere? Why was he fixed, immoveable, plodding out his life like a magnificent ox? Why did he wear Hera's yoke? And for the first time he thought it was his own yoke he wore.

He looked up at the stars. There was the constellation of Cancer, another of his enemies elevated by Hera. A giant crab had nipped him in the foot while he was battering the Hydra. He had crushed the crab, but for his pains, there was his foe glittering at him, uncrushable forever.

Cancer the Crab. The zodiac sign of Home.

'Go home, Heracles' . . . no, he would never go home. It was too late.

★   ★   ★

Heracles got up from under the tree, and taking Ladon's lopped off tail, scrambled over the wall of the garden and made his way back to Atlas. On the way he caught a sleeping forest pig, and carried it with him to cook and eat. Outwardly, he was still Heracles, bluff, ready, direct, untroubled. Inwardly, some part of him was riven – not by doubt – he did not doubt what he must do, but by a question. He knew *what*, he no longer knew *why*.

Thought-Wasp

Which is what he said to Atlas when they ate together under a wedge of stars.

'Why are we doing this, mate?'

'Doing what?'

'You're holding up the Kosmos and I'm spending twelve years clobbering snakes and thieving fruit. The only good time was chasing Hippolyte, Queen of the Amazons, and she didn't want anything to do with me when I caught her. Independent women are like that. I don't know which is worse – the dependent ones who bleat at you all day, or the bitches who couldn't care less.'

'What happened to Hippolyte?'

'I killed her of course.'

'I knew her once.'

'Sorry mate.'

There was a pause. Atlas was silent. Heracles drank another skinful of wine. He didn't want to think. Thinking was like a hornet. It was outside his head buzzing at him.

'What I mean to say, Atlas, is why?'

'There is no why,' said Atlas.

'That's just the trouble,' said Heracles. 'There is a why, here, or here, or here,' and he started hitting the side of his head, trying to squash the droning thought.

Atlas said —

'Bent under the world like this, I hear all the business of men, and the more I hear them questioning their lot, the more I know how futile it is. I hear them plan for tomorrow and die during the night. I hear a woman groaning in labour and her child is stillborn. I hear the terror of the captured man, and suddenly he is set free. I hear a merchant travelling home from the coast with his goods, and robbers set upon him and take all he has. There is no *why*.

There is only the will of the gods and a man's fate.'

'I'm the strongest man in the world,' said Heracles.

'Except for me,' said Atlas.

'And I'm not free . . .'

'There is no such thing as freedom,' said Atlas. 'Freedom is a country that does not exist.'

'It's home,' said Heracles. 'If home is where you want to be.'

Then Heracles tried to throw off his dark mood.

'So you think you're stronger than I am, do you Atlas? Can you balance Africa on your dick?'

Atlas started to laugh, which was unfortunate for the earth, experiencing this as a deep tremor. Heracles already had his own dick out and was working it furiously to make it stand.

'Come on, stick it on here. Let's have the whole continent smack on my bulb.'

'You're drunk,' said Atlas.

'I saw Hera this afternoon. God what a ball-breaker.

You know that story about the Milky Way and how it was the milk I spurted out after she suckled me? Well it wasn't the milk, it was this stuff, but she's too much of a lady to tell anyone.'

Heracles was just about to come. 'This'll put snow on the Himalayas, eh boy?'

He lay back, scattered over the stars. 'Go on Atlas, now you.'

'I don't have a free hand.'

'I'll do it for you if you want – mate to mate.'

'I'm too tired.'

'You sound like a girl.'

'You should try holding up the world.'

'I've told you, I'll do it tomorrow. On my nose, like a seal.' He started to snore.

'Good night Heracles,' said Atlas, though there was no reply.

Heracles's snoring thundered over the world below, while Atlas gazed out, as he always did, into infinite space, wishing he could be part of it, even for one hour.

Morning came to test Heracles's promise. There was the tricky question of how Heracles could physically take the Kosmos from Atlas without dropping it. After some discussion it was agreed that Heracles would slide himself up Atlas's back, like a mating snail, and pull the world down onto his own shoulders.

It worked well enough, except that the gods themselves were overturned in their beds, and a meteor the size of a town crashed to earth, sinking part of Sicily.

Atlas felt his gigantic burden slip from his body, and he turned to thank Heracles whose face was red as a pomegranate, his muscles hard-braced as stone.

'It gets easier,' said Atlas.

'Just go and get the apples,' was all the response Heracles could manage.

★   ★   ★

Atlas rubbed his legs and lower back. He had forgotten what standing upright felt like. He stretched his arms above his head, hearing the crack of stiff joints and enjoying the slow easing off of dorsal and trapezius. He trod through the heavens, kicking the stars like stones. He stepped down out of the clouds the way a man steps out of a mist. He was back on earth. He was proportional and seemly. His gigantic nature was contained. He was looking for his garden and he found it.

When Atlas pushed open the heavy peeling wooden door, some of his high spirits were checked. What time had failed to ruin, Heracles and Ladon had achieved. The ground was scorched and polluted from the serpent's fiery venom. The wall was down where Heracles had kicked it scrambling over. The cloches and the frames and the stakes and the wires that had trained the apricots to the wall were all broken. What fruit was left was run wild and eaten up by maggots or birds. The good soil that he had dug and sieved was thick with matted grass. His shed had a hole in the roof.

The garden seemed to represent the loss of everything that had mattered to Atlas; his daughters, his peace and quiet, his own thoughts, his freedom, his pride. Angrily, he grabbed a rusty billhook and when he had cleaned it on his leather belt and sharpened it against a stone, he began to cut back the wasted garden.

By evening there was a great stack of dead branches and unwanted growth and Atlas set it alight like a funeral pyre. The flames scorched up high, even Heracles could feel them on his neck and he wondered what Atlas was doing. The dense smoke offended the gods, who knew that this was no sacrifice, and Zeus himself decided to intervene. He crept into the garden disguised as a rough old labourer in a donkey skin.

'Is Lord Atlas returned to The Garden of the Hesperides?'

'Who are you?' said Atlas, piling nettles onto his fire.

'My name is Parsimonius. I have little to spare and little to share but I will help you if I can.'

'How can you help me?' said Atlas.

'I can warn you that it was Zeus who ordered your punishment and Zeus who will enforce it.'

'You seem to know a lot about Zeus,' said Atlas.

'I am a religious man.'

'Most mean men call themselves so – it excuses their own behaviour.'

'How will you excuse your own behaviour?'

'You can tell Almighty Zeus that his bastard son Heracles is holding up the world.'

Zeus knew nothing of this, or of the encounter with Hera in the garden. Like most women, Hera was careful not to tell her husband everything.

'Heracles has his own punishment to bear.'

'He is able enough to bear his own and mine for a while. Besides he wants to think.'

Now Zeus was anxious. Real heroes don't think.

'What is Heracles thinking about?'

'You want to know a lot for a donkey skin don't you?' said Atlas, who was beginning to suspect his visitor's true identity. 'I'll tell you for what it's worth – Heracles is thinking about himself. Yes, Heracles, born with rocks for muscles and a rock between his ears, asked me last night why he should do the gods' bidding. I thought it was a stupid question, hardly a question at all, but it's the first question that Heracles has ever asked, other than *Which way?* and *Are you married?*'

'What did you answer?' asked Zeus.

'I made no answer. If there is no question there can be no answer. No one can ask *why* to the gods.'

Zeus was relieved by this remark. He did not doubt that even if Heracles was thinking now, he would not be thinking later. What he feared was that Atlas might begin to consider the nature of Heracles's blind question.

'You answered well, Atlas. I am sure that Zeus will overlook this small excursion.'

'I am sure Zeus knows nothing of it,' said Atlas.

'Perhaps you are right. Some questions are best not asked at all. If I were asked now, "Where is Atlas?" I should say, "in his usual place".'

Parsimonius got up from the tuft where he had been sitting, and bowing to Atlas, left the garden. As soon as he had gone out of the door, Atlas used his arms as jack-levers and heaved himself up the wall so that he could watch his visitor's path. Parsimonius had vanished completely, but for a small trail of golden-ish dust.

'That was Zeus alright,' thought Atlas to himself, and something troubled the giant, though he did not yet know what it was.

Meanwhile, Heracles was not happy. The world was much heavier than he had guessed. His strength lay in action not in endurance. He liked a short sharp fight, a good dinner and sleep. His body was as strong as Atlas's, but his nature was not. Hera was right about him there. Heracles's strength was a cover for his weakness.

Nobody argues with a man who is twice as tall, twice as heavy, twice as hot-tempered, and three times the big head. Argue with Heracles, and he'd crush you. So he was always right. If he took his chariot in to be fixed, it was 'Right away Mr Heracles, we weren't busy, we'll do it now,' and the long line of chariots waiting to have their axles repaired could moulder to dust, while Heracles's special racing model was brought to the front of the line.

The garage fixed the wheel and cleaned the chariot for free. Heracles used the riding box like a horse-drawn dustbin, and it was always full of discarded wineskins and yesterday's quick-shot boar.

No matter.

Heracles would sit on a straw bale and look at drawings of nymphs while the chariot was made useful and beautiful again. Sometimes people would come and ask for his autograph, and he'd scrawl his name with a bone on a wax tablet. He never paid for anything, and if anyone challenged him, he killed him. His life was simple. He was a simple boy. Women, like wood, were for splitting and for keeping him warm. He loved to divide a woman's legs and push himself inside her. No woman ever refused him. That was his charm.

That was his story. No woman who ever refused him lived to tell the tale. Hippolyte had almost got away with it. He had felt pity as he stood over her exhausted body. He had pursued her for a year – or was that Artemis's hind? He couldn't remember. It had been a long tiring run though, he knew that, and she was the only woman who could out-distance him. She would have got away if some friends of his hadn't ambushed her in the mountains.

As he stood over her, his sweat plopping onto her face, he had wanted to lift her up gently and share his food with her. He thought of marrying her. He asked her if she'd marry him, as he stood there swinging his club. She said something about Amazons never marrying. Something silly like that, and he realised she was just a woman like the rest, who would never know what was good for her. He hesitated, and then knocked off her head the way you open a desert cactus.

Blood covered his feet. There was some there still, caught under his toenail, a tiny dye-marker of the kind that rich people used to mark their possessions from thieves.

Poor Heracles. Hera's milk and Hippolyte's blood. A man bonded by women.

Then Heracles had a very unpleasant thought. *Suppose Atlas never came back?*

Three Golden Apples

In his garden, Atlas went to pick the three golden apples.

As his hand went towards the first, he felt a rumbling under his feet, and he had to steady himself against the tree. The tree bark was cool as silver, though the apple dropped into his hand like molten gold. It was as if somebody else had picked the apple and given it to him. Uneasily he looked around. There was no one there. There was only the cool night.

Atlas put the fruit into his pocket and made for a second, perfect apple. This time he heard a groan, distinctly, a groan, and felt a terrible pain in his chest. He staggered slightly, bruising his back against the tree, while an apple, whole and unmarked, rolled down his body to where he caught it in his hand. There it was, in the palm of his hand, a little world complete unto itself.

For a long time, Atlas gazed at it, and he thought he could see continents under its skin, and the rush of rivers that flowed from one country to another. He laughed, and he felt affection, and pride, and that unbearable tightening in his chest again. He wanted to cry, his tears pouring over the apple, like rain.

He was not used to feeling. He saved himself in his lonely hours by thinking. He invented mathematical puzzles and solved them. He plotted the course of the stars. He tried to understand the ways of gods and men, and was mentally constructing a giant history of the world. His thoughts kept him from dying. His thoughts kept him from feeling. What was there to feel anyway – but pain and weight?

Now, gazing at this tiny world, he felt an emotion he hardly recognised. He did not dare to name it.

★ ★ ★

Heracles, his strength bound without motion, was having a panic attack. He was alone. There were no fires, no lights, no cooking smells. There was no one to listen to his stories, or to get drunk with, or to praise him. His only company was the hornet buzzing outside of his head, the thought-wasp, buzzing Why? Why? Why?

In the garden, Atlas put away the second apple and reached for the third. There was a crashing around his head, and a saw of lightning, as yellow as the apple, cut the third fruit from the very top of the tree and hurled it at him. Atlas stretched to catch it, and hit the ground. The apple was heavy as thought. It lay beside him in the grass and try as he might, he could not pick it up.

Atlas was scared. Like all the sons of Mother Earth, his strength was renewed when he came in contact with the ground. His brother Antaeus had been in hand to hand combat with Heracles, and for a long time it looked as though Antaeus would win, for every time Heracles wrestled him to the ground, Antaeus sprang up again with new strength.

Heracles, who could be smart when his life was at stake, finally realised that he must hold Antaeus above his head and crack his ribs. It worked.

But now, Atlas was in his own element and he couldn't manage to pick up an apple. With huge difficulty he rolled it towards him, and lay looking at it, beside his head.

His forced exile had taught him to concentrate. He used to go about the world as busy as a man could be, organising, building, farming, making his wine, selling it, supplying jewels to the wealthy, talking with the powerful. He had been one of the powerful.

A powerful man doesn't notice much. He doesn't need to. Other people notice things for him.

Atlas, alone in the cosmos, keeper of the world, had learned to interpret every sound, every sign. He knew when there would be a storm or an earthquake. He smelled the burning waste of collided stars. He understood even the smallest sounds – a man turning over in bed, a bird calling danger when a hyena passed. He listened to rocks compress creatures into fossils. He heard the crack of tree-fall, as men cleared the forests.

Now, lying with his face in the grass, he heard angry shouts from Tartarus, where the dead are, where some of his own brothers were, hating death, wanting life, crowded in a limbo of eternity, longing for time.

There had never been enough time for all the things Atlas liked to do, and now that he was immortal, he had only the punishment of forever. Forever to be the same person. Forever to perform the same task.

He listened. He heard a woman pounding beetles to make purple dye. She would do that forever wouldn't she? That was her work, and though she might spend the evenings eating and drinking and singing and visiting her friends, her life would never change.

Did she care? Atlas listened to hear if she sighed — no she did not sigh — she hummed as she pounded, and her mind was elsewhere, on her lover, on her children, on the pleasure of a warm day.

Would he now, this minute, change his life for hers, give her the world and pick up her pestle and mortar?

He deceived himself. When he cried for any relief from his monstrous burden, he did not really mean it. He was still Atlas. He was Lord of the Kosmos, wonder of the universe.

His punishment was a clever one — it engaged his vanity.

He looked at the apple. For the first time he began to think that he had colluded in his punishment. Why had he fought against the gods? He already had more than enough. He had a kingdom, he had power. True that the gods had stirred up the Athenians against Atlantis, but what had the war achieved? His beautiful cities and harbours were sunk. His palace was decorated with fishes. There was no such place as his world.

Why had he not recognised the boundaries of his life, and if he had recognised them, why did he hate them so much?

Always boundaries and desire . . .

It is fit that a man should do his best and grapple with the world. It is meet that he should accept the challenge of his destiny. What happens when the sun reaches the highest point in the day? Is it a failure for morning to become afternoon, or afternoon to turn into peaceful evening and star-bright night?

Heracles was more afraid now than he had been in his whole life. He could accept any challenge except the challenge of no challenge. He knew himself through combat. He defined himself by opposition. When he fought, he could feel his

*muscles work and the blood pumping through his body. Now
he felt nothing but the weight of the world. Atlas was
right, it was too heavy for him. He couldn't bear it. He
couldn't bear this slowly turning solitude.*

In the garden, Atlas became aware of another pres-
ence. Veiled Hera was standing by her tree.

'Atlas,' said Hera, 'why do you lie there?'

'Are you sent to punish me?' said Atlas.

'Pick up the apple,' said Hera.

'I can't.' Atlas laughed. His position was ludicrous.

'Atlas, do you know what this tree is?'

'It is your tree, given to you by Mother Earth.'

'And what is Mother Earth's greatest gift?'

'Knowledge of past and future,' said Atlas.

*Earth is ancient now, but all knowledge is stored up in her.
She keeps a record of everything that has happened since time
began. Of time before time, she says little, and in a language
that no one has yet understood. Through time, her secret*

codes have gradually been broken. Her mud and lava is a
message from the past.

Of time to come, she says much, but who listens?

'The apples you have taken are your own past and
future,' said Hera.

Atlas was afraid. His future was at the ends of his
fingers, and too heavy to be moved.

'The third apple is the present,' said Hera, 'made
from your past, pointing towards your future. Which
is it Atlas? Only you can decide.'

'Why could not Heracles pick the fruit himself?'

'Heracles stole from me once. He will not steal
from me again.'

'Why did you send Ladon to guard the tree?'

'Anyone who plucks these apples will be like the
gods, knowing past and future as though they were
today.'

'That would be a blessing for mankind.'

'That would be a curse,' said Hera. 'Humankind

continues in ignorance because knowledge destroys them. Everything that man invents he soon turns to his own destruction. Your brother Prometheus stole fire and what did men do with that gift? They learned to burn each other's crops and houses. Chiron taught you medicine and what did you learn to make? Poisons. Ares gave you weapons, and what did you do with them but kill each other? Even you, Atlas, half man half god, destroyed the most beautiful city in the world. You preferred to ruin your own farms than see them harvested by another. You scuttled your own ships rather than see them in the hands of the enemy.'

'The gods made war on us,' said Atlas.

'So you made our job easy and wiped yourself out.'

'Why do you talk like this?'

'To help you make a choice.'

'I have no choice.'

'That is what you said when you made war on the gods.'

'There is no choice. There is Fate. No man escapes his fate.'

'Look at the tree Atlas.'

Atlas rolled on his side and looked at the tree, strangely shining. He could not count the fruit.

'You chose three apples. Did you choose them by accident or chance?'

'When I looked there were only three apples on the tree.'

Atlas was puzzled. He had seen the tree laden with fruit, just as it was laden now, but while he had been picking the apples, there had seemed to be only three, the three he had to choose.

'There was no enchantment, Atlas. You could not see the tree as it is. You could not see the change-fulness of the world. All these pasts are yours, all these futures, all these presents. You could have chosen differently. You did not.'

★ ★ ★

Atlas said, 'Must my future be so heavy?'

Hera said 'That is your present, Atlas. Your future hardens every day, but it is not fixed.'

'How can I escape my fate?'

'You must choose your destiny.'

Dark-minded Hera vanished and Atlas was alone. He held the apples lightly in his hand. He had no idea what Hera had been telling him, he hardly knew whether he cared. He had to go back to Heracles now, and his only plan was to persuade the hero to hold up the world for a little longer.

No Way Out . . .

Heracles was asleep.

He dreamed he was a single moment in a single day. A note struck and sounded. Gone. He was the chime of Ladon's scales. He was the whistling hiss of the Hydra. He was the hoof-beat of Artemis's hind. He was a cattle bell, he was the bottom G of the boar, he was the singing sound of Diomedes's mares, he was the operatic shriek of the Stymphalides, he was the bass of the Nemean lion, the bellow of the Cretan bull. He was the noise of running water through the Augean stables, he was the whimper of a dog, he was the sigh of a dying woman.

Then he was himself, and he was tearing at his flesh as though it were a shirt he could pull off. He was the sound of his own agony.

He woke in a sweat. He couldn't even wipe his brow. He stared unfocussed into the serene starryness of the universe and wondered if he shouted loud enough would he get a reply?

There was no noise. There was a noise and he hated it. The buzz, buzz, buzz outside his head.

'ATLAS' he yelled 'ATLAS' and on earth there was thunder in the mountains.

'There's no need to shout,' said Atlas. 'I can hear you.'

There he was, tall, smiling, standing in front of Heracles, blissfully free of any burden. Heracles felt his skin burning with jealousy.

'Did you get the apples?' he said, trying to sound cool.

Atlas reached into his pouch pocket and brought them out, still shining with their strange light. Then he said,

'Heracles, I'll take these to Eurystheus for you.'

'Wouldn't hear of it mate,' said Heracles. 'You've done enough already.'

'It's no trouble,' said Atlas.

'You don't want to go all that way just to deliver a few bits of fruit.'

'I thought I might visit my daughters too,' said Atlas.

('Bloody hell,' thought Heracles, 'those girls will keep him forever.')

'You aren't getting tired are you?' Said Atlas.

'Tired? No mate, I love it here, makes a change, no problem.'

'Well then,' said Atlas, 'do you want anything before I go?'

Heracles was nervous. If he made a fuss, Atlas could just walk away. Heracles couldn't put the world down without help. Atlas could trap him here forever.

★　★　★

'Since you ask, I'd like a pad for my head – take the weight off. Bloody Switzerland.'

'What's wrong with Switzerland?' Said Atlas.

'The mountains mate. They're sticking in the back of my neck.'

Atlas was kind hearted and he did not want to see Heracles suffer, so he searched through his bag of belongings and found a thick fleece that he could fold into a cushion. He bent over Heracles and tried to fit it behind his neck.

'Matterhorn mate . . .'

'What?' said Atlas.

'You'll never get it under the Matterhorn. Look, just take the world for a second, and I'll fit the pad on my shoulders, and then we'll be straight. Oh and don't squash the apples will you?'

Unsuspecting Atlas nodded and bent down to put the apples on the floor of the universe. Then with a light flick he spun the Kosmos off Heracles and held it over his head.

Heracles quickly picked up the apples.

'Better make yourself comfortable mate. I'm not coming back.'

For a second Atlas did not speak. Then as he studied Heracles's grinning face, he realised he had been tricked. Wily Heracles had no brains but plenty of cunning.

What could Atlas do? He wanted to hurl the universe at Heracles, crush him, annihilate time and make the story start again.

'Come on Atlas,' said Heracles, 'you've had your fun.'

Slowly, so as not to spill one drop of milk, Atlas lowered the Kosmos back onto his shoulders, and bent himself under the burden. He did it with such grace and ease, with such gentleness, love almost, that Heracles was ashamed for a moment. He would gladly have dashed the world to pieces if that would have freed him. He saw now that Atlas could do just that, but did not, and he respected him but would not help him.

'Goodbye Atlas,' said Heracles, 'and thanks . . .'

Heracles turned away in his lion skin, swinging his olive club, the apples at his belt by his side. As he pushed the stars out of the way and began to fade though the warp of time, Atlas saw his past, present and future, disappear with him. Now his life had no demarcations, no boundaries. There was nothing, and wasn't nothing what he had wanted?

But why was nothing as heavy as nothing?

He turned his head, and just for a moment he didn't see the universe balanced there on his back. It was himself he was carrying, colossal and weighty, little Atlas desperately holding up the Atlas of the world.

Then the vision was gone.

But Through

Heracles delivered his apples to Eurystheus.

Glad to be rid of his grocer-duties, he struck south, and founded the hundred-gated city of Thebes, in honour of his birthplace.

Honour or not, birthplace or not, Heracles soon tired of being a city-dweller. Leaving behind his fine clothes and all-night feasts, he dusted out his lion skin (now a little threadbare), and travelled until he came to the Caucasus Mountains. Here, Prometheus had been chained alive for more time than anyone could remember.

Heracles knew he was close to Prometheus's rock-face prison, when he saw the griffon-vulture circling overhead in the first light of morning. Every morning the vulture tore out Prometheus's liver, and every night, his liver grew back again, so that he should never escape punishment for stealing fire from the gods.

Not wishing to be seen, Heracles hid behind a rocky outcrop, and watched as the vulture swooped closer and closer. Its curved beak began to graze, then puncture, the pale flesh of Prometheus's stomach.

His face creased in agony, yet not crying out, Prometheus flattened his back while the vulture ripped open his stomach muscles and put its whole head into the man's gut to tug out the liver. While it rummaged there, it flapped its great wings to keep airborne, and used the man's hipbone as a perch for its claws.

The liver hanging half in and half out of the bloody wound, the bird gave a fierce pull, and Prometheus cried out. The liver dangling from its beak, the vulture flew straight upwards, dripping spots of blood and tissue onto the stained rock.

Prometheus fainted.

Heracles came out from his hiding place and held

a skin of water to Prometheus's lips. Prometheus revived and thanked Heracles, and out of pity Heracles covered the wound from the blinding sun and the flies that tormented Prometheus through the day.

Prometheus asked Heracles if he had seen his brother Atlas, and Heracles suddenly remembered the manner of infinite gentleness with which Atlas had resumed the impossible burden of the world. Gently, Heracles wiped Prometheus's brow and promised to intervene with Zeus that day for an end to the punishment.

Good as his word, he set off, leaving his water flask and a reed straw.

When Heracles wanted something he usually started by shouting for it.

'ZEUS! FATHER ZEUS!' His voice rolled round the mountains, slipping boulders and sending small rocks tumbling into crevasses.

Zeus was with Hera, in an intimate moment, on a golden couch, and Hera, raising one eyebrow and smiling to herself, pulled Zeus back towards pleasure.

Heracles was getting angry. If shouting didn't get him what he wanted he used his club, and so he ran to the top of the highest mountain, careless of the blazing sun, and began to hammer on the sky.

The gods felt the commotion and some wondered if the giants were attacking them again. Hermes was sent to discover the source of the riot, and when he saw Heracles threatening to split the sky in two, he agreed to take him to Zeus's palace.

Zeus knew nothing of this until Heracles opened the bedroom door and found his father on top of his stepmother. Hera turned her beautiful head towards Heracles and gave him that ironic look that he hated, while his prick went kangaroo.

As Zeus withdrew himself from Hera and covered her up, he said to Heracles,

'What do you want with the gods?'

'Pardon Prometheus,' said Heracles. 'He has suffered enough.'

'Mercy from a murderer,' said Hera, without looking at him, 'Well well.'

Now Zeus had long repented of his punishment to Prometheus, and he was glad of an excuse to pardon him. But not even a god can go back on his word, and so Zeus had to change the punishment from a reality to a symbol. Prometheus must wear a ring made out of his chains, and set with a stone from the Caucasian Mountains. Heracles was to kill the griffon-vulture with an arrow.

'You'll enjoy that won't you?' said Hera, sweeping by him in a silk shift and stroking his unshaven cheek with a hand that smelled of myrrh. When she had left the room, Zeus shrugged his shoulders and patted his rough son on the back, as if to say,

Women, what can you do with them?

All night Heracles sat by Prometheus until his wound closed over, just before dawn. Prometheus was heavily sunburnt, but his stomach was pale like a child's because the skin was new every day.

As Heracles dozed, his dreams were filled with the beating of wings and a scorching in his body. He dreamed he was carrying the world again, but the world had a sharp beak and talons and savaged him wherever he stood. Again he tried to tear off his flesh as though it were a shirt.

He woke up with no time to lose. The vulture was upon Prometheus, it's beak already scoring a thin red weal across his stomach. Heracles aimed his arrow and shot the bird in the throat. It fell in vast circles, down and down the unscaleable rocks and into a dry gully too far away to see. Heracles snapped Prometheus's chains with his bare hands, and laughing and crying, Prometheus followed him down the mountain to a great feast held in his honour by the men for whom he had stolen fire so long ago.

Zeus himself appeared at this feast in his usual guise of the stranger. Hera sent her apologies. She had a headache.

Zeus had brought Heracles's arrow with him and he set it in the heavens as the constellation Sagittarius. Heracles was flattered by this especially because it was Hera who always raised up his enemies into the stars. He felt that Zeus had at last acknowledged him. He felt he was at last being rewarded, instead of punished, for the hero, the conqueror, the *good man* that he was.

Prometheus came to Heracles out of the shadows of the fire.

'Heracles, you have saved me and I thank you.'

'I would save you again, a thousand times,' said Heracles.

'Then save my brother Atlas. Ask Zeus for his pardon too.'

Heracles smiled and nodded and turned back to the fire and the feasting. He would not save Atlas, no matter how much he pitied him, because there was the only man who could take his burden, and Heracles would never do that again.

He looked up and saw Zeus the Stranger gazing at him keenly as if he knew his thoughts.

Heracles looked away and all he seemed to see in the fire was Hera's mocking smile.

Leaning on the Limits of Myself

What can I tell you about the choices we make?

Fate reads like the polar opposite of decision, and so much of life reads like fate.

When I was born my mother gave me away to a stranger. I had no say in that. It was her decision, my fate.

Later, my adopted mother rejected me too. And told me I was none of her, which was true.

Having no one to carry me, I learned to carry myself.

My girlfriend says I have an Atlas complex.

When I was small, my bedside lamp was a light-up globe. Accrington wasn't on the map, and England, hardly so, but the seas of the world seemed infinite, and I thought I could sail them until I came to a better place; a place that would be a *yes* and not a *no*.

When I was smaller than small, in the orphanage, the room outside my window had a big globe pendent light, made of white china. It looked like the moon. It looked like another world.

I used to watch it until the image of it became sleep, and until the last tram whooshed past, the bend in the road made audible by the air concertina'd in the rubber pleats.

The globe and the tram were my companions, and the certainty of them, their unfailingness, made bearable the smell of sour milk, and the high bars of the cot, and the sound of feet on the polished lino, feet always walking away.

I am good at walking away. Rejection teaches you how to reject. I left my hometown, left my parents, left my life. I made a home and a life elsewhere, more than once. I stayed on the run. Why then, did the burden feel intolerable? What was it that I carried?

I realise now that the past does not dissolve like a mirage. I realise that the future, though invisible, has weight. We are in the gravitational pull of past and future. It takes huge energy — speed-of-light power — to break that gravitational pull.

How many of us ever get free of our orbit? We tease ourselves with fancy notions of free will and self-help courses that direct our lives. We believe we can be our own miracle, and just a lottery win or Mr Right will make the world new.

The ancients believed in Fate because they recognised how hard it is for anyone to change anything. The pull of past and future is so strong that the present is crushed by it. We lie helpless in the force of patterns inherited and patterns re-enacted by our own behaviour. The burden is intolerable.

The more I did the more I carried. Books, houses, lovers, lives, all piled up on my back, which has always been the strongest part of my body. I go to the gym. I can lift my own weight. I can lift my own weight. I can lift my own weight.

I want to tell the story again.

Private Mars

Atlas was watching Mars.

Mars has no life. It has an atmosphere of a kind, thin and volatile, and its surface is home to dust storms and hurricanes.

The surface of Mars has no soil; it is covered in something called *regolith* – a mixture of dead rocks – some boulders, some pebbles. They formed valleys and causeways and there were signs that water had once flowed through them, aeons ago.

There is no water now. At least not on the surface. Underneath the surface is permafrost a mile deep. Below that are aquifers of brine with a freezing point of minus twenty centigrade.

Some afternoons, on Mars, the weather is as sunny as Australia. By night, the carbon dioxide lies in mists of dry ice in the bottom of the arid valleys.

What would it take to melt the ice and free the water?

What would be needed for a single plant to grow?

Atlas, the gardener, sometimes imagined himself smashing deep wells into the unconscious frost, and reviving life on the sun-abandoned planet. He would shovel away the regolith and bring in fertile soil. Soil is the active surface of a living planet. He would lie in the dirt and dream.

His dreams were always the same; *boundaries, desire*.

In the limitless universe of his imagination he would not be punished for wanting the impossible. Why did the gods insist on limits and boundaries when any fool could see that these things were only rules and taboos — customs made to keep people in their place? Rebellion was always punished like this — by taking away what little freedom there was, by encasing the spirit.

He thought of the East and all those geniis in jars. Dangerous things have to be contained. He was a dangerous thing and his body was held prisoner so that his mind should not escape.

They had got it the wrong way round, of course. His mind was always escaping. They had captured his body, but not this thoughts.

Yet he had made a garden, and his occupation now was imagining another garden, difficult and fantastical, made from nothing and brought to life. He would wall it just as he had walled the Hesperides, and he knew that his happiest time was inside those self-made walls.

True and not true.

His walls, his door in the wall, and always half open when he was inside. Only locked when he had gone. He jealously protected his boundaries from intrusion by others – that was why he had gone to war against the gods in the first place – though they would say he had invaded what belonged to them. Demarcation, check-points, border controls. And all in the name of freedom. Freedom for me means curbing you.

Atlas knew, because he was not stupid and because he had all the time in the world, that something was missing from his argument. He had known it that day with Hera when he picked the apples. He had known it as something growing inside him ever since.

Boundaries. Desire.

He turned over the words like stones. The words *were* stones, as dry and inhospitable as the Martian regolith. Nothing grew out of those words. It was these he would have to break open and crumble into good soil. It was these he would have to water and watch and sleep beside for the first sign of life.

His own private Mars. That was where he lived now. The garden was gone.

Hero of the World

Heracles often thought of Atlas . . .

Atlas, lonely, aloft, holding up the Kosmos, like a boy with a ball.

Heracles never visited Atlas again, some combination of shame and fear kept him away. He had cheated to win, he knew that, but how could he blame himself? Blame Hera. Blame the gods for setting him impossible tasks; tasks that any other man would have failed.

Time faded the insult. The thought-wasp hardly stung him at all now. Only sometimes was there that buzzing discontent that made him want to tear his head off and discus it into space.

He had other things on his mind now. He was getting a new wife.

★   ★   ★

Deianeira was the kind of woman everybody wanted. She was the daughter of Dionysus, and had all his extravagance. She had a body like a feast, skin as smooth as wine, an appetite for pleasure, and she could go all night. She was perfect for Heracles.

He wooed her in his usual way with a lot of bragging and a few tricks with his biceps. He promised to take her travelling with him. He needed a wife and he had no legitimate children left alive. The ones he hadn't killed himself by mistake, others had killed for him. Besides, it was prophesied that if he did not die within the next fifteen months, he would live out his days in quiet happiness.

It was time to settle down.

Some time after the marriage, the two of them were travelling together, happy and intimate, when they came to a fast-flowing river. As they were wondering how to cross, the centaur Nessus galloped up and offered to carry Deianeira on his back, while Heracles swam across.

Carefully, Heracles lifted his wife onto the centaur's hairy back. Instead of plunging into the water, Nessus made off with Deianeira, and took her into his woods where he intended to rape her.

Heracles chased in pursuit, and stringing his bow, shot Nessus in the chest from half a mile away. The centaur was on his forelegs over Deianeira's naked body, prick dripping on her belly, when the arrow hit him. He fell down on her and as he died he told her that to make amends he would offer her a charm. Collect his semen, mix it with blood from the arrow tip and use it to keep Heracles faithful forever. That's all she had to do. He was sorry. Goodbye.

Deianeira recovered her wits and the mix of fluids, just before Heracles came thundering up to yank Nessus off her body and pitch his corpse into the bushes. He was so upset at his wife's naked condition that he made love to her himself, his head buried in her shoulder, her hair over his neck.

Deianeira lay with her eyes open, feeling him and looking at the fast-moving clouds. Heracles could never be still. There was always another woman; a fling, a whore, a mistress, a bar-girl, a prize, a ransom, a spoil from a fight, a farmer's daughter, a goddess. Heracles had never promised to be faithful. It was neither his nature nor his inclination. Deianeira had assumed she wouldn't care. They were married, he honoured her publicly, he was the father of her children. He liked her. Yes, they got on well, which was new for Heracles, and surprising for Deianeira. She could handle a chariot, she was good on a horse and she could partner him at target practise. He admired her. He could talk to her. This was the best ever for Heracles. He thought she knew that. He thought it was enough.

In a way it was enough, but when she looked at herself in the watery mirror, it was age she feared. How could she keep him when her body was no longer like a flowing stream? In a few years, other men would no longer want to violate her, they would hardly

notice her. Heracles would rid himself of her the way
he rid himself of anything in his way. Deianeira did
not know of the prophecy. She did not know that
she was the one.

She was the one.

Some time later Heracles went to collect a bet.

Heracles never forgot or forgave an insult. Before
he had met Deianeira, he had hoped to marry Iole,
daughter of King Eurytus. He had won her fair and
square in an archery contest, but her father had
refused to give her up. Heracles, married or not,
regarded Iole as his.

It was a typical day in the life of a hero. He took
Deianeira tea in bed, gathered his army, and went to
lay waste to Eurytus. Soon the city was burning, the
inhabitants had been put to the sword, and Heracles
stormed the royal palace, where he began to slit the
throats of all Iole's family. Everytime he caught one,

male or female, he held a dagger to their throat and shouted 'Iole! Say you'll be mine and this one lives!'

Rather than yield to Heracles, Iole watched her entire family being murdered. Then while Heracles was gutting her last remaining brother, she fled to the top of the city walls and flung herself off.

Heracles dropped the half-dead body and ran out to see what was happening. Instead of hurtling her body to ruin, Iole was drifting gently down the ramparts. Her skirts had made a parachute of her fear. Heracles caught her in his arms as she reached the earth, one hand moving straight between her legs. As he carried her over his shoulder, his prick bursting, he massaged her cunt with his dirty bloody finger, and made her wet. She had never felt anything like this before, and by the time he threw her onto his couch on the boat, she was kissing him as passionately as he kissed her. She was tight and ready and he loved it. This one he was going to keep.

★　★　★

When Deianeira got to hear of his doings, she felt pity and not resentment for Iole, but when she heard that Heracles wanted to bring Iole to live with them, her pride burned.

Iole was much younger than she. Iole was in love with Heracles, or thought she was. Heracles was besotted with his new toy. Life would be intolerable for Deianeira, and if she complained, well, Heracles would ignore her or leave her.

Message came that Heracles wanted to sacrifice to Zeus before returning home. He asked Deianeira to send him a new shirt to wear for the sacrifice.

This was her moment. She remembered the words of Nessus, and locking the door to her room, she took his potion out of her secret safe in the wall.

The square of wool was still as soaked and wet as on the day she had used it to collect the blood and sperm. There was no smell or heat to it. She had every reason to believe she had been deceived, but it seemed like her only chance, and so she rubbed the cloth carefully over Heracles's new shirt and left it to dry.

Heracles was in bed with Iole when the shirt arrived. He left the girl sleeping and went outside in the cool clear morning, which seemed strangely precious to him that day.

He built a vast altar to Zeus and rounded up twelve bullocks which he killed with his bare hands and prepared for the sacrifice.

He would go home after this. He would reconcile Deianeira to Iole. He would be happy. A wife, a mistress, plenty of children, plenty of wine, a reputation, and at last some peace. He might even build himself a garden.

He suddenly thought of Atlas, star-silent. For a second, the buzzing started again, in the usual place, by his temple. He hit his head. The buzzing stopped.

★   ★   ★

Deianiera had packed the shirt. She went up to her room and lay on the bed Heracles had built for them. The sun came through the window, and suddenly she smelt a foul burning. Looking on the floor, she saw that a tiny piece of the soaked wool had been left behind. The sun had heated it and now it had turned into a scorching, suppurating mass. Gas bubbles burst from it, and the smoke from the poison was filling the whole room.

As Deianeira staggered out, she realised that Nessus had deceived her. The shirt would not bind Heracles to her, it would kill him.

She summoned her fastest courier and sent him after the shirt. She vowed that if Heracles died, she would not survive him. She began to sharpen a knife.

Heracles had made ready the altar. He lit the sacred flames and stepped back to put on clean clothes. A servant gave him the fine shirt that Deianeira had sent, and he blessed her as he wore it, vowing to himself that he would give up Iole if that was what Deianeira wanted. He realised how much he loved her and he had never loved anyone before. Iole was gorgeous, but she was just a girl. He could get another one of those.

He stepped forward to pour frankincense on the flames, tall as towers. In his reverie he did not hear the great commotion among his servants behind him. Deianeira's courier had arrived and was trying to break through to Heracles, while the servants held him off. There was a shout, 'HERACLES!' but it was too late. As Heracles turned, the flames caught his shirt and began to release the terrible poison. As Heracles roared and tried to pull off the shirt, it clung closer to him, and it was skin he pulled away, in roasting seared slices.

No man shall kill Heracles, but a dead enemy.

He remembered the prophecy. As he ran demented to the sea, he shouted his wife's name over and over, and she heard him and knew what she had done, and took the knife and stabbed herself through the heart.

And Hera, far away, smiled her ironical smile. He had killed himself after all. She knew he would.

Woof!

Atlas heard of the death of Heracles. It was the last thing he heard from Olympus.

No one told him the old gods had vanished or that the world had changed through a pale saviour on a dark cross.

Time had become meaningless to Atlas. He was in a black hole. He was under the event horizon. He was a singularity. He was alone.

The planet Mercury takes only eighty-eight days to orbit the sun, but a single day on Mercury lasts as long as one hundred and seventy six earth days. A Mercurial year is only half a day. Time passes slowly and quickly here.

So it was for Atlas, for whom forever and never had become the same thing. He was part of the galaxy now, part of a celestial city of millions or billions of stars, gas and dust-bound together by their gravitational pull.

In this vast city no two clocks kept the same time. It was impossible to make an appointment. While Mercury flew round the sun in days, Saturn took nearly twenty-nine years. And there were other planets now, unknown to the Greeks. Jupiter, Neptune and Pluto made time a watchword for mortals only. A single year on Pluto counted up two hundred and forty eight of the earth's. Pluto, Lord of the Underworld, was in no hurry.

Atlas did not know how long he had been here.

Then the dog came.

She was a good dog, a faithful dog, a trusting dog, who loved her master and obeyed him when he put her inside a tiny capsule and strapped her so that she could not move. She was afraid but she believed in him. She was his dog.

When the Russians blasted Laika into space in 1957, they knew she wasn't coming back. An automatic hypodermic would poison her after seven days. She would orbit in her sputnik until the universe stopped.

When they closed the lid on Laika she trembled and her mouth went dry. There was water in a tube and she had been taught to drink from it. There was food too, but she didn't want water and food, she wanted her master, and night, and quiet, and all this not to be.

She was patient. She would have gone to the ends of the earth for her master. Instead she went into space.

Atlas had retreated so far into his mind that he did not notice the strange pod buzzing round him. Then he saw a little face at the thick sealed window. For a moment his heart leapt. Was it Heracles? Heracles transformed into his own thought, the only one he had ever had, the *why* question that he had silenced by hitting his head against as many brick walls as he could find.

As the pod came round again, Atlas freed one of his hands from his monstrous burden and caught it. It lay there like a lamed insect on his palm, and there was something inside.

Atlas cracked open the sputnik and found Laika, strapped down, unable to move, partly bald with fear and covered in sweat and urine and her own faeces. With infinite care, Atlas freed the dog, and set it down safely on nothing and gave it water to drink.

The speck-sized dog in the star-stretched universe licked the giant's hand. At that moment the needle in the pod moved to inject its victim, but it was too late. Laika was free.

Atlas knocked the pod aside, the silly thing of tin and wires, and Laika crawled unsteadily up his arm until she found a place to sleep, in a hollow of his shoulder under the wavelength of his hair.

Atlas had long ago ceased to feel the weight of the world he carried, but he felt the skin and bone of this little dog. Now he was carrying something he wanted to keep, and that changed everything.

Boundaries

Friday, March 23rd 2001, 5:49 a.m., Pacific Ocean.

The Mir space station came home.

The Russians had loved Mir. They kept it up there through hardship and poverty, paying the bills with blustering loans and black market dollars. Since the days of the first Sputnik, the Russians loved space. It didn't belong to America. It might one day belong to them.

It was the same old story — *boundaries, desire.*

When Mir crashed into the Pacific at dawn, she landed history but the dream escaped. There it is, orbiting the world, gravity free. Free as a dream should be.

What kind of dream?

We dream we're free.

★   ★   ★

The earth's atmosphere extends for about a hundred kilometres above the earth's surface. Travel upwards just a couple of miles, and you can escape gravity. Here there is no weight, only a measureless sea of space-time.

Here we are, one of nine planets revolving round a nuclear star in a spiral arm of a minor galaxy. Our sun is a hundred and fifty million kilometres away. Pluto, the outermost of the nine planets, lies six billion kilometres away from the same sun. This tiny, icy planet of change and death has never been visited, and the Greeks couldn't see any further than Saturn. Saturn, for them, and for astrologers still, was the planet of limitation. This was the *so far and no further* planet, the warning, the boundary.

Now it seems there are no boundaries. The universe has no centre. Every limit can be crossed. Even the speed of light – 300,000 kilometres per second – is not the speed limit of the universe. If we could warp space, we could break the light barrier.

One day we'll do it all.

For now, we've landed on the moon and we've sent BEAGLE 2 to Mars. We know so much more than Mir. We know more about outer space than anyone ever. But all we know is just the start. These are jottings, hesitations, small facts, big gaps.

Like all dreams, the details are strange.

Atlas would miss Mir. He had been watching it for years. They both watched it. It was television for him and the dog.

Laika had told Atlas all about the world he had never seen. Of course, her world stopped in 1957, and it was the Soviet Union, so Atlas thought that everyone now ate beetroot and turnip and shivered in zero temperatures in concrete apartments.

The dog said that the earth was full; soon its inhabitants would have to live in space. Atlas had got used to his own company, and he didn't want humans he had never met flying round his face in their tinny pods. He was a prisoner but he had rights.

They had both seen the moon landing in 1969. Atlas assumed that the men wore those ridiculous clothes because it was so cold on earth these days. He thought of the sun warming his garden, and how he had always gone barefoot. Laika assured him that no one went barefoot in Russia.

'Where is Russia?' said Atlas.

'Over there,' said Laika, wagging her tail.

Atlas looked round at the jigsaw of the earth. The pieces were continually cut and re-cut, but the picture stayed the same; a diamond blue planet, ice-capped, swirled in space. Nothing was as beautiful. Not fiery Mars nor clouded Venus, not the comets with their tails blown by solar winds.

Then Atlas had a strange thought.

Why not put it down?

Desire

What can I tell you about the choices we make?

I chose this story above all others because it's a story I'm struggling to end. Here we are, with all the pieces in place and the final moment waiting. I reach this moment, not once, many times, have been reaching it all my life, it seems, and I find there is no resolution.

I want to tell the story again.

That's why I write fiction – so that I can keep telling the story. I return to problems I can't solve, not because I'm an idiot, but because the real problems can't be solved. The universe is expanding. The more we see, the more we discover there is to see.

Always a new beginning, a different end.

★   ★   ★

When I was a kid my parents were still living in the war.

My father had been in the D-Day landings. My mother was a young woman in 1940. They adopted me late in life, and I was raised among gas-masks and rationing. They never understood that the war was over. They remained suspicious of strangers, and kept themselves closed off in the personal air-raid shelter they called home.

My mother had a war-time revolver she hid in the duster drawer, and six bullets waxily embedded in a tin of furniture polish. When things were bad, she took out the gun and the polish and left them on the sideboard. It was sufficient.

On revolver nights, I crept to bed and switched on my light-up universe. I used to travel it, country by country, some real, others imagined, re-making the atlas as I went.

My journeys were matters of survival; crossing nights of misery into days of hope. Keeping the light on was keeping the world going. It was a private vigil, sacred to stop things falling apart – her, me, the life I knew – however impossible – the only one.

Looking at the glowing globe, I thought that if I could only keep on telling the story, if the story would not end, I could invent my way out of the world. As a character in my own fiction, I had a chance to escape the facts. There are two facts that all children need to disprove sooner or later; *mother* and *father*. If you go on believing in the fiction of your own parents, it is difficult to construct any narrative of your own.

In a way I was lucky. I could not allow my parents to be the facts of my life. Their version of the story was one I could read but not write. I had to tell the story again.

I am not a Freudian. I don't believe I can mine the strata of the past and drill out the fault-lines. There has been too much weathering; ice ages, glacial erosion, meteor impact, plant life, dinosaurs.

The strata of sedimentary rock are like the pages of a book, each with a record of contemporary life written on it. Unfortunately the record is far from complete . . .

My mother said we all have our cross to bear. She paraded hers like a medieval martyr, notched, gouged, bleeding. She believed in Christ, but not in his cross-bearing qualities.

She seemed to forget that he had borne the cross so that we don't have to. Is life a gift or a burden?

What is it that you contain?

The dead. Time. Light patterns of millennia opening in your gut.

Your first parent was a star.

I know nothing of my biological parents. They live on a lost continent of DNA. Like Atlantis, all record of them is sunk. They are guesswork, speculation, mythology.

The only proof I have of them is myself, and what proof is that, so many times written over? Written on the body is a secret code, only visible in certain lights.

I do not know my time of birth. I am not entirely sure of the date. Having brought no world with me, I made one.

Spin the globe. What landmasses are these, unmapped, unnamed? The world evolves, first liquid and alive, then forming burning plates that must cool and set. The experiment is haphazard, toxic at times. Earth is a brinkmanship of breathtaking beauty and a mutant inferno. My own primitive life forms take a long time to web intelligence. When they are intelligent they are still angry.

For me, still, now, anger is deeper than forgiveness. My red-hot monsters aren't extinct. I've kept their Jurassic forest, hidden but complete. They're still there, jawed, plated, furious. The sky is purple-brown.

I am, of course, homo sapiens, at least on paper.

Spin the globe. If oxygen falls below fifteen percent of air volume, I can hardly move. If it rises above twenty-five percent, I and my world conflagrate. Homeostasis of my planet is hard work. I swing between one extreme and another, constantly threatening my stability. I am always in danger of self-destruction.

Breathe in. Breathe out. Oxygen is carcinogenic and likely puts a limit on our life span. It would be unwise though, to try to extend life by not breathing at all.

Which of us doesn't do it? Either we loll in anaerobic stupor, too afraid to fill our lungs with risky beauty, or we roll out fire like dragons, destroying the world we love.

I try not to burn up my world with rage.

It is so hard.

★ ★ ★

Spin the globe. When I made it, it was small as a ball. I carried it on a stick over my shoulder. I was the fool, new and careless. I didn't know that worlds are on the Planck scale – infinitesimally tiny, exploding to grow.

It grew. It utilised free energy from the sun. It learned to break the oxygen-carbon compounds. It started a life of its own.

I used my world like a crystal ball, gazing into it, looking for clues. I loved its independence, the unknownness of it, but like everything you birth, it gradually becomes too big to carry.

It's on my back now, vast and expanding. I hardly recognise it. I love it. I hate it. It's not me, it's itself. Where am I in the world I have made?

Where in the world am I?

About five billion years ago, the material that now makes up the sun and the planets was a great cloud of dust called the Solar Nebula. This material was a mixture of light elements, like hydrogen and helium, along with heavier elements thrown out by an earlier generation of brief stars. A shock wave or an exploding star prompted the nebula to condense into a galaxy of proto-stars.

In one of these proto-stars, material concentrated to form the proto-sun. Gas and dust around it collected into a flat rotating disc. Over the next thousand years or so, the disc cooled, and grains of solid matter began to freeze. In the hot inner region, they were silicate rocks. Further out, there was watery ice, and further out yet, frozen methane. These grains moulded themselves into mile-long lumps, bumping, breaking, colliding, but sometimes co-operating to form the planets.

The four planets closest to the Sun – Mercury Venus, Mars and Earth – are small rocky worlds. The next four planets, Jupiter, Saturn, Uranus and Neptune, are gas giants. Pluto is more like a moon than a planet. There is no life except here. Planet Earth. *The Almost, the Proto, the Maybe.* Planet Earth, that wanted life so badly, she got it.

Beside me, the lamp still glows. Here I am, turning and turning the lit-up globe, leaning on the limits of myself.

What limits? There are none. The story moves at the speed of light, and like light, the story is curved. There are no straight lines. The lines that smooth across the page, deceive. Straightforward is not the geometry of space. In space, nothing tends directly; matter and matter of fact both warp under light.

If only I understood that the globe itself, complete, perfect, unique, is a story. Science is a story. History is a story. These are the stories we tell ourselves to make ourselves come true.

What am I? *Atoms.*

What are atoms? *Empty space and points of light.*

WEIGHT

What is the speed of light? *300,000 kilometres per second.*

What is a second? *That depends where in the Universe you set your watch.*

Let me crawl out from under this world I have made. It doesn't need me any more.

Strangely, I don't need it either. I don't need the weight. Let it go. There are reservations and regrets, but let it go.

I want to tell the story again.

I want to tell the story again

Long ago, this violent planet of radioactive rock had learned to become home.

Atlas had loved the earth; the crumble of soil between his fingers, the budding of spring, the slow fruit of autumn. Change.

Now the earth changed but Atlas had stayed still, feeling the tilted axis rotate against his shoulder blades. All his strength was focussed into holding up the world. He hardly knew what movement was any more. No matter that he shifted slightly for comfort. The monstrous weight decided everything.

Why?

Why not just put it down?

★　★　★

Atlas let his hands go from the sides of the world. Nothing happened.

Atlas put his hands down in front of him on the floor of the universe or the ceiling of stars, I don't know which, and then he stretched out his left leg so that he was kneeling on all fours, the Kosmos balanced on his back. Laika was running in and out of his spread fingers. She had never seen her master move.

Atlas crawled forward and then suddenly fell flat on his face with hands over his ears and the dog clinging on to his thumb. Atlas waited, rigid with doom. The dog waited, her nose in her paws.

Nothing happened.

Write it more substantially – NOTHING.

Atlas raised his head, turned over, stood up, stepped back. The dog's nose lifted. Atlas looked back at his burden. There was no burden. There was only the diamond-blue earth gardened in a wilderness of space.

All that we can see is only a fraction of the universe.

Some matter is detectable only by its gravitational effects on the rotation of galaxies. This is called dark matter and no one knows its composition. Dark matter could be conventional matter, like the small stars called Brown Dwarfs, or it could even be black holes.

Or it could be Atlas holding up the universe.

But I think it is Atlas and Laika walking away.

JEANETTE WINTERSON's first novel, *Oranges Are Not the Only Fruit*, won the Whitbread Prize for Best Novel. Since then, she has published seven other novels, including *The Passion*, *Written on the Body*, *The PowerBook* and *Lighthousekeeping*, a collection of short stories, *The World and Other Places*, a book of essays, *Art Objects*, and most recently, a children's picture book, *The King of Capri*. She has adapted her work for TV, film and stage. Her books are published in thirty-two countries. She lives in Oxfordshire and London.